LITTLE OLEG

MARGARET & JOHN CORT

Hodder Children's Books

Once upon a time there were two friends, called Eric and Oleg. They lived in a northern country. Eric's house was large and he had several acres of land. Oleg's house was small and all the land he owned was his vegetable garden.

Oleg was a most agreeable person. For example, if his friend said the moon was made of green cheese, he would agree with him, even though he knew that it was made of Gouda.

One night, Oleg was awakened by a banging at his door. He thought he was dreaming and settled down further into his blankets. It was a cold night and the freeze was just setting in.

But the banging continued,
and Oleg realised that there
really was someone there.

It was his neighbour Eric.
'Come quickly!' he was shouting.
'My house is on fire. My house is on
fire and you do nothing but sleep!'

Oleg rushed to put his coat on. Eric sank into an
armchair and fanned himself. 'Run!' he said. 'I shall
follow as soon as I get my breath back.
I am quite worn out...'

Little Oleg ran all the way...

But when he reached the house he saw that
nothing could save it. He dragged out all he
could until he was overcome by smoke and
had to give up. His coat had caught fire
and there were great holes burnt in it.
Sadly he returned home.

Eric was asleep in the chair where he had left him. He woke up when Oleg entered. 'I must have fallen asleep. What a terrible night! Now I have no home... Oh! What shall I do?' He began to cry.

'Please don't cry, Eric,' said Little Oleg. 'You must stay with me until the thaw, and then I will help you to build a new house. Sit there and I'll get you something to eat.'

There was just enough food for one in the cupboard. Eric gobbled the food and did not notice that Oleg was not eating.

The days passed and Oleg began to get short of flour. He had laid in a stock for the winter, but it was not enough to feed two men (one of whom had a very large appetite).

Oleg went to the miller and asked him
to let him have another four bags of flour.
He promised he would sell his vegetables in
the spring and repay him. The miller agreed,
although he knew that little Oleg usually
ate all the vegetables he grew.

The two friends continued to live in perfect harmony. Eric sometimes felt irritable. He was not used to living in such a small house, and Oleg's bed was not as comfortable as his own had been. But then the thaw came and they were able to start building the new house.

They worked for weeks and weeks and, at last, it
was ready. It looked splendid and Oleg felt proud,
as he had done most of the work.

'Of course,' said Eric, 'it's not as grand as
my old house, but it will do.'

Eric seemed to be happy there, however, for he seldom left it to visit Oleg, who was now hard at work in his garden trying to make up for lost time.

It was a bad season, and as Oleg had not been able to get an early start, his crop was a failure. There would be no vegetables to sell. With a heavy heart little Oleg set off for the mill again.

The miller was very sympathetic, but he was short of money, too.

'Well, Oleg,' he said, 'I would like to help you but I only grind the meal, you know. I have to buy my grain from the farmers and they must have cash. I am putting a new wheel in my mill. The workmen must be paid, or their families will starve. The children will throw stones at my windows and shout that the miller grows fat while they grow thin… for I am fat, although I can't help it… In fact, it's a disadvantage, as you would know if you had ever been the fat one on a see-saw…'

Oleg could see that somehow he would have to repay the miller at once.

On the way home Oleg decided to go and see if Eric could help him. Eric was eating his supper.

'I wish I could help you,' he said. 'If it hadn't been for that fire you would have no need to worry. As it is I am a ruined man... almost. But wait!'

While talking he had noticed Oleg's ragged coat. He had often been ashamed of his friend's appearance, but this was too much. His coat looked for all the world as though it had been through a fire. He had been wanting to get rid of an old coat, but had not liked to offer it to Oleg before. However, since the fellow had come back to talk about his poverty, he could hardly be offended.

'Here is a coat which belonged to my father,' said Eric. 'See what you can do with it. Yours is a disgrace.'

As Eric watched his friend go, he began to regret giving him the coat. 'I am too soft-hearted,' he thought. 'I should have given him a lecture instead.'

'I suppose I could ask the tailor what to do
with this coat,' said Oleg glumly to himself,
'though my old coat is the least of my worries.
There is only one thing to do. I shall have to sell
my house – and then I shall have nowhere to live.'

Oleg found the tailor in his shop. 'Eric gave me this coat,' he said. 'Do you think I could cut it down and make it fit?'

The tailor looked closely at the coat. 'I made that coat for Eric's father thirty years ago. These buttons are gold,' he said. 'They are wasted on it now. If you want to sell them I will buy them from you.'

'Would you?' cried Oleg. 'Of course, I should have to give the money to Eric.'

'Nonsense!' said the tailor. 'He gave you the coat, didn't he? He would have taken the buttons off if he had wanted them. It looks as though he decided to do you a good turn at last.'

'A good turn? Of course. He didn't mention the buttons in case I would be embarrassed,' said Oleg. 'What a good friend he is!'

'This is a stroke of luck for both of us,' said the old tailor as he snipped them off. 'I am making a coat for a rich gentleman at the moment, and he is most particular about buttons. I'll give you twenty crowns for the lot.'

TWENTY CROWNS!

Little Oleg could hardly believe it.

He hurried off to the mill. When the miller

had taken what was owing, they found

Oleg still had ten crowns left.

Then Oleg had a wonderful idea. He would give a party for Eric. The miller must come and bring his wife. The tailor, too. He ran from door to door, asking all who could to come to his house that night. He bought good things to eat and drink, and soon there was hardly any money left. There was only one more thing to do and that was to tell Eric about the party.

Eric did not look very pleased when he heard there was to be a party. 'Party?' he said. 'Waste of money! Besides, I thought you were hard up?'

'Well, I was,' said Oleg, 'but the tailor gave me twenty crowns for the gold buttons on your father's old coat. I am giving a party for you, because you have been so kind to me.'

'GOLD BUTTONS? What are you talking about?' cried Eric.

'Why, the buttons on the coat you gave me,' said Oleg. Oleg looked puzzled. 'You will come to the party?' he asked. 'All our friends are coming to eat and drink your health.'

'Party? Certainly not!' said Eric. 'I don't feel well. I shall have to go to bed,' and he shut the door.

'FOOL!' Eric shouted. 'Twenty crowns for those lovely buttons. I should have got twice as much from that old rogue... if only I had known.'

The thought of half the village eating and drinking at his expense was enough to make Eric weep. When night came he sat by the window, his face a picture of misery. He was all alone. Down the hill at Oleg's house everything was as merry as could be.

Only Oleg seemed to notice that Eric was not there. 'He must be lonely,' thought Oleg. 'He may be rich, but poor Eric has no friends.'

Oleg put aside some choice dainties, and when the last guest had gone he slipped away up the hill to Eric's house and laid the parcel at his door.

Then, feeling happier than he had done for
many a day, little Oleg hurried home to bed.

For Susan

HODDER CHILDREN'S BOOKS

First published in 1965 by Brockhampton Press Ltd.
This edition published in 2016 by Hodder and Stoughton.

A CIP catalogue record for this book is available from the British Library.

ISBN: 978 1 444 92205 9

1 3 5 7 9 10 8 6 4 2

Printed and bound in China.

Hodder Children's Books
An imprint of Hachette Children's Group
Part of Hodder and Stoughton
Carmelite House
50 Victoria Embankment
London EC4Y 0DZ

An Hachette UK Company
www.hachette.co.uk
www.hachettechildrens.co.uk

MIX
Paper from
responsible sources
FSC® C104740